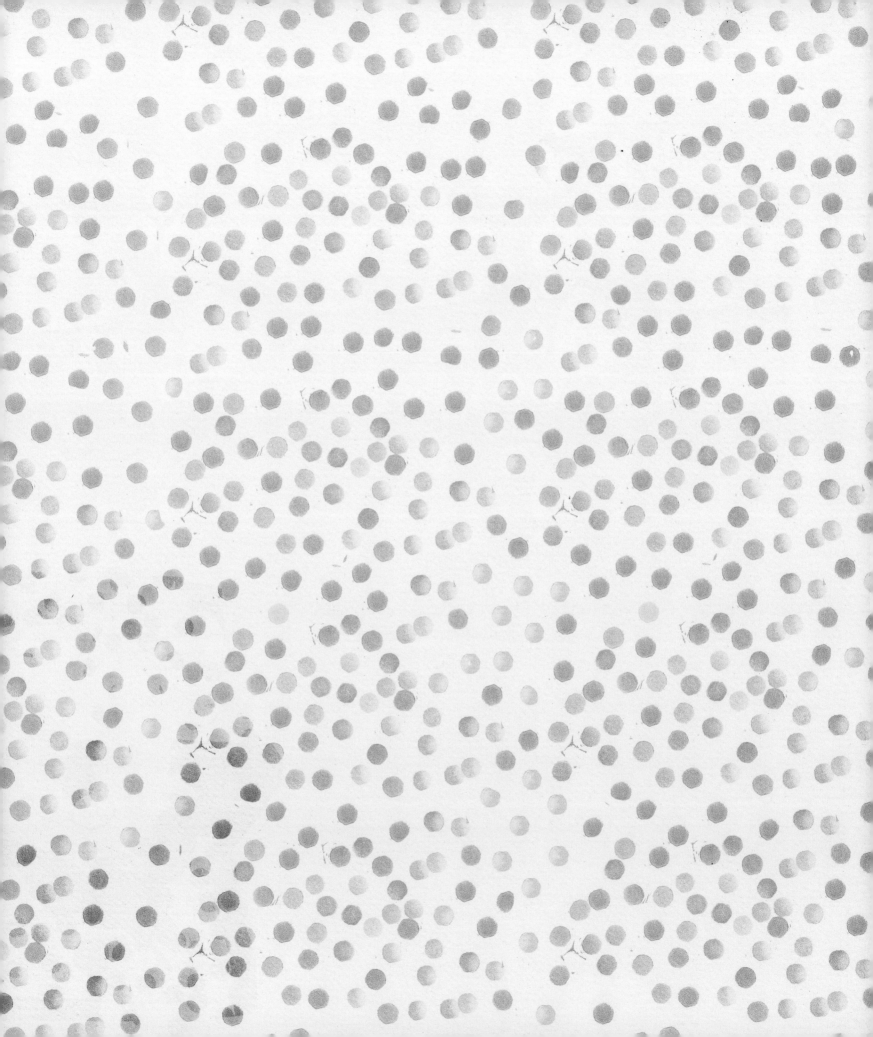

For Max,
I love you to the moon and back x

EGMONT
We bring stories to life

First published in Great Britain 2018
by Egmont UK Limited,
The Yellow Building, 1 Nicholas Road, London W11 4AN
www.egmont.co.uk

Text and illustrations copyright © Gwen MIllward 2018

Gwen Millward has asserted her moral rights.

ISBN 978 1 4052 8682 4

A CIP catalogue record for this title is available from
the British Library

TIGER LILY

Gwen Millward

EGMONT

"Tiger did it," said Lily.

"Tiger is very naughty," said Penny.
"Where is he?"

"Hiding," said Lily.

And it was true –

Penny couldn't see
Tiger anywhere.

But Lily knew he was there.

The next day, the special strawberry fairy cakes Penny had baked disappeared.

And then something happened to Penny's knitting.

"Did Tiger do that as well?" asked Penny, crossly.

"Yes," said Lily. "And he **isn't** sorry," she added. Which was true, he wasn't.

"Well, Tiger is **very** naughty and will go to his room until he says he's sorry," said Penny.

Tiger was listening.
He didn't like being told off **at all**.

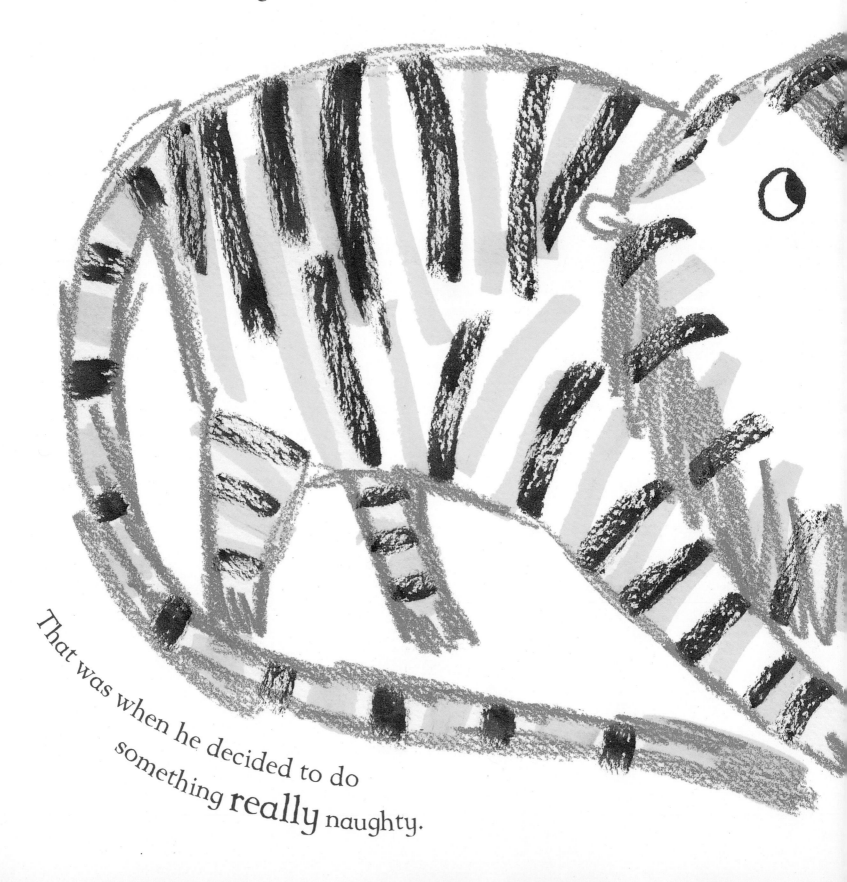

That was when he decided to do something **really** naughty.

"Come on, Lily,"
roared Tiger. "Let's run away
and have some fun. We can
do anything we want. We can be

Wild!"

Lily knew running
away was bad.
But she did it anyway.

She tiptoed out of her bedroom
and packed a bag of important things:

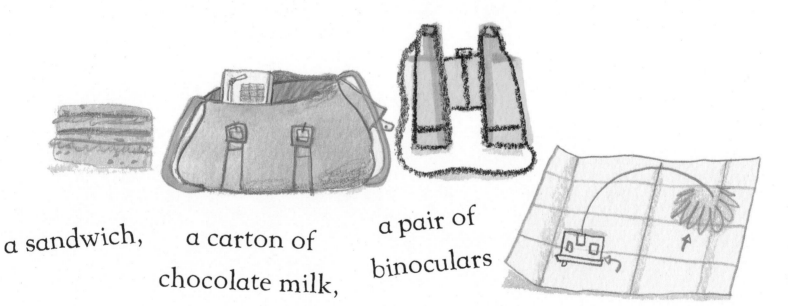

a sandwich,   a carton of
                chocolate milk,

a pair of
binoculars

and a map, so she could
find her way home.

"Let's go!" shouted Tiger.
"Let's stomp and jump and make a mess!"
Tiger wanted to do everything...

So they did.

They **stomped** through the long grass.

And they **jumped** in muddy puddles and made a big mess.

The wild was **good.** Tiger and Lily felt free.

There was no one around to tell them off.

"Follow me,
Lily!" said Tiger,
leading her deeper into the wild
where the bushes grew thick.

Sometimes there were big scary
things, and Lily was glad to have
Tiger, who was never afraid.

But other times . . .

she wished he wasn't quite
so roarsome and wild.

On and on they went, and Lily began to feel hungry. She reached into her bag for her sandwich . . .

but it wasn't there.

Tiger looked at Lily.

Lily looked at Tiger.

And then Lily realised . . .

the sandwich
was in Tiger!

So was the
chocolate milk
and the binoculars!

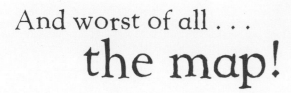

And worst of all . . .
the map!

"I'll never find my way back!" cried Lily.

But Tiger thought **that** was a good thing.

"We can be **wild forever!**" he roared.

And then Tiger did something **really** bad . . .

he **ate** Lily's shoes!

"Stop it, Tiger! You're **too** naughty! Go away!" shouted Lily.

She didn't want to be wild forever. So she ran.

Lily missed Penny. She knew Penny would be missing her too, even if she was still cross.

It was getting dark.
Scary night things
were about.

The wild was getting **wilder**
and Tiger was nowhere to be seen.

In fact, Tiger didn't seem to be there at all.
Suddenly Lily heard a rustle in the grass.

But it **wasn't** Tiger . . .

It was Penny.

They hugged.

Then hugged some more.

"Tiger shouldn't have taken me into the wild
without telling you," said Lily, "and Tiger is sorry."

And he was VERY sorry.

"He's sorry for being naughty, too," said Lily.

And he was.
Very, very sorry.

"Can we go home now?" asked Lily.

So they did.

Penny wrapped Lily in a big blanket.
And Lily wrapped up Tiger next to her.

After that day, Tiger and Lily did sometimes go to the wild together. But they never went for long. And they never went without telling Penny.

And sometimes . . .

Penny went too, because the **wild** can be **fun** and **good** for

everybody!

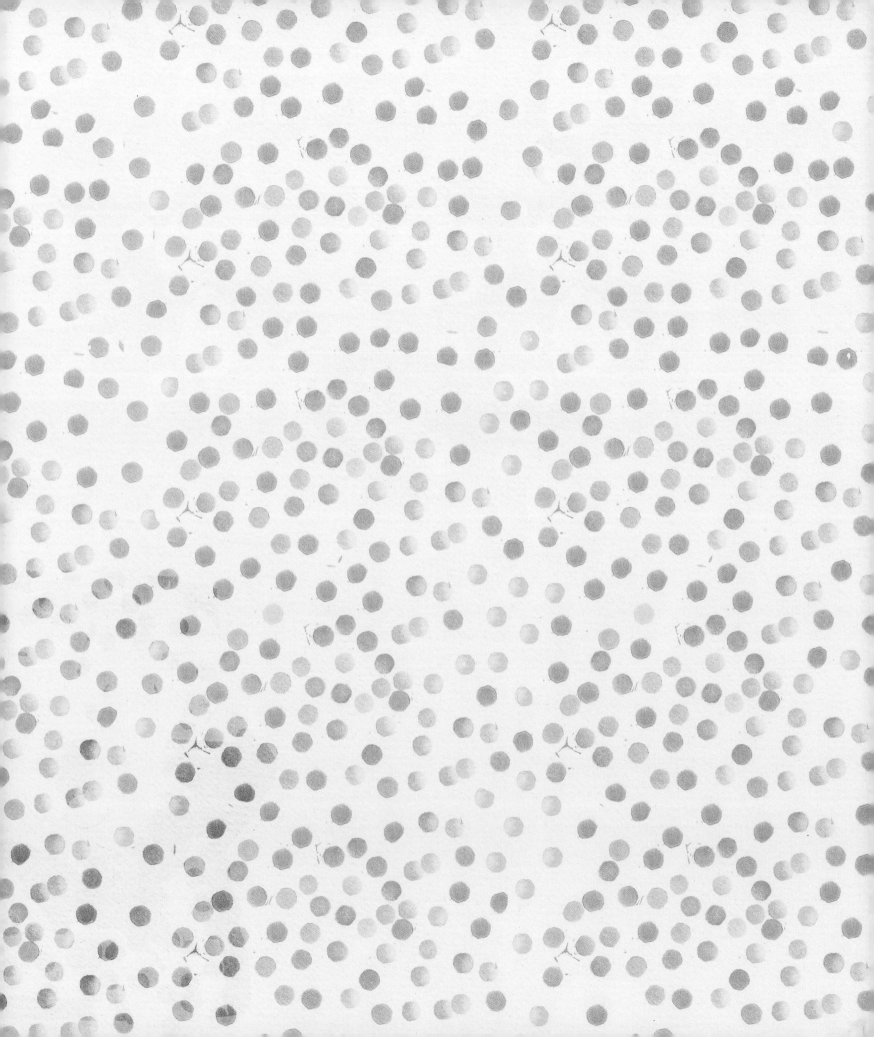